This igloo book belongs to:

....

"Hello, I'm Ellie.
Let's have fun being
fairies together!"

Published in 2011
by Igloo Books Ltd
Cottage Farm
Sywell
NN6 0BJ
www.igloo-books.com

L006 0811

2 4 6 8 10 9 7 5 3 1

ISBN: 978-0-85734-814-2

Printed and manufactured in China

Ellie's Magic Wish

Alice King

Illustrated by
Kate Daubney

igloo

I want to be a fairy
and sit on mushrooms, drinking tea.

I'll ask my other fairy friends
to come and visit me.

If I were a fairy,
I'd have shiny, silky wings.
I'd flit around the forest
and twirl in fairy rings.

If I were a fairy,

I'd wave my magic wand.
I'd make a sparkly, golden boat
and sail around our pond.

I want to be a fairy,
so I can fly up high.

I'll wear my silver wings
and swoop across the sky.

I want to be a fairy
and bake proper, fairy cakes.

I'll make them extra sticky-sweet,
like the ones that Grandma makes.

If I were a fairy,
I'd make lots of magic wishes.

I'd make my bunny talk to me
and give me lots of kisses.

I want to be a fairy
and have a secret den.

I'll sprinkle it with fairy dust
and visit, now and then.

If I were a fairy,
I would meet the Fairy Queen.
She'd tell me that my pretty dress
was the best she'd ever seen.

I want to be a fairy
and dance to fairy tunes.

I'll be a fairy ballerina
and twirl under the moon.

If I were a fairy,
I'd fly around at night.

I'd flit among the flowers
and shine my lantern light.

If I were a fairy,

I'd ride a magic unicorn.
He would glow like moonbeams
and have a golden horn.

I want to be a fairy
and make my wand go, swish!

Maybe, if I'm very good, one day I'll get my wish!

"Goodbye!
Remember to sparkle!"

Watch out for more fantastic stories in the igloo picture book range!

Detective Ted

An ordinary teddy turns detective to solve the mystery of who is eating all the cookies at night.

Fly, Freddy, Fly

There are thrills and spills galore in this touching story about a penguin who is desperate to fly.

Rosy's lost Balloon

A moving story about a little bear who loses her precious balloon, but finds a happy ending after all.

igloo